If I Were a Dog

JOANNA COTLER

PHILOMEL

Thank you, Jill, Elena, Laura, Jay, Ellice, China, and Jasmine.

PHILOMEL BOOKS

An imprint of Penguin Random House LLC, New York

First published in the United States of America by Philomel, an imprint of Penguin Random House LLC, 2021.

Visit us online at penguinrandomhouse.com.

Library of Congress Cataloging-in-Publication Data is available.

Manufactured in China

ISBN 9780593116104

10 9 8 7 6 5 4 3 2 1

Edited by Jill Santopolo.
Design by Ellice M. Lee.
Text set in Print Bold OT.
The art in this book was created with watercolor.

For my sweet sisters, Amy and Ellen

If I were a dog . . .

I'd be silly, just like me.

Or patient, just like me.

I'd be nosy

or shy.

Just like me.

Sometimes
I'd be
grumpy.

Sometimes I'd be happy.

I might look big,
but I'd feel small.

Or I might look small, but

I'd feel **big.**

WOOF WOOF

WOOF WOOF

I might be noisy.

Or quiet.

Maybe I'd run faster than anybody.

Or maybe not.

Like me.

I'd be so playful . . . .

sometimes I'd get into trouble.

(So much trouble.)

Just like us.

If I were a dog, I'd worry,
but no one would know.

Sometimes I'd be

touchy

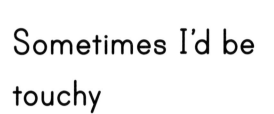

or lonely.

I might have sisters
and brothers

and a friend or two . . .

or seven.

And we could cuddle and
be sleepy together.

No matter what, I know
if I were a dog, I'd be loved . . .

just like me.